This book belongs to

To my children Aaron, Lili, & Colette—
you are my greatest reflection.

-Ariel

Sapphire Publishing, LLC

Text and Illustration © 2022 by Sapphire Publishing, LLC
First edition

ISBN
979-8-9867636-0-6 (Hardcover)
979-8-9867636-1-3 (Paperback)
979-8-9867636-2-0 (eBook)

Library of Congress Control Number: 2022915057

Edited by: Brooke Vitale
Designed by: Arlene Soto

Printed in China

Follow us at @Sapphire Storytime on Instagram and Facebook
Sapphire Publishing LLC offers discounts for purchases of larger volumes.
Supplemental educational and teaching material can be provided as well.
For more information or inquiries, please contact ariel@sapphirepub.com, or visit sapphirepub.com

Neela's Reflection

written by
Ariel Zylberberg

illustrated by
Eduardo Paj

Out past the lake, on a warm summer night,
Deep in the forest, the sky glittered bright.
The fireflies came when the skies all grew dark,
To light up the grass blades, the leaves, and the bark.
In green, red, and orange, they lit while they flew—

That is, all but one, who just glowed a dull blue.
No matter the task, or the challenge or sport,
Poor Neela, it seemed, always came up just short.

She stared in the lake, with a grumpy, mean pout,
And said to herself, "Things don't ever work out!

There was that one time that I cooked a souffle,
Or put on a tutu and danced a ballet.
Singing a song wasn't quite a success,
And building sand castles is always a mess!"

And as she looked down, from her point of view
She looked even smaller, and a shade paler blue.

Now Neela felt tired and full of frustration

As three 'flies approached, in a perfect formation.

They blinked all at once; in a straight line they flew.

"**That's great,**" Neela grumbled, "**more things I can't do.**"

Gracie glowed green; she was smart as a whip.
Zigging and zagging, she flew with some zip!
She'd tell you the facts, and then make up some more,
On beetles, or birds, or a large dinosaur.

Michelle lit up orange, was strong, and had sass—
With spunk and a spirit no one could surpass.
While Daniel shined yellow, and liked to relax—
To swim in the lake, with some worms as his snacks.

The three seemed quite happy, but Neela just stewed,
As Gracie approached her to brighten her mood.
"Why sit here and mope, all alone on the shore?
There's so much to see and so much to explore!

We're off to go searching for bright, shooting stars,
To look up and fly among Venus and Mars."

It all sounded fun, Neela had to admit,

It had to be better than wanting to quit.

Maybe she'd try just one final time . . .

She thought as she gathered her courage to climb.

She headed straight up, with her heart full of glee

Until she felt . . . SPLAT!! . . . and crashed in the tree!

She fell to the ground, with
wet tears down her face,
To looks of great shock from
both Daniel and Grace.

She wibbled and wobbled
as she flew away,
"Don't go!" cried Michelle,
"there's a storm on the way!"

She made her way back to her spot by the lake,
Her ego was battered, her head had an ache.
So down in the dumps, and filled up with dejection,
She looked down to see her imperfect reflection.

A strong, gusty breeze, made her pause and then stop—
She felt on her head just a single rain drop.
The one turned to two and then two drops to three,
As Neela raced back to hide out in the tree.

Loud thunderous **BOOMS** made the whole forest shake!
As raindrops bombarded and smashed in the lake.
The dark clouds rolled in, while winds from the North
Caused all the wet branches to sway back and forth.

Neela hid out as the storm reached its peak—
Until she was shocked by a loud, piercing **shriek!**
For Daniel had made a most dreadful mistake
And found himself stuck, under rocks, past the lake.
He'd ventured too far in the hopes of a snack,
But now found himself with no way to get back!
Neela sought help, by the shore, on the ground,
But try as she might, there was none to be found.
Not foxes, or frogs, or a firefly light
Was there to help Daniel come out of his plight.

With fear in her heart, but a spark in her eye,
Neela exhaled and looked up to the sky.

With no one around, there was no other choice.
She yelled, "Hang on tight!" in her bravest, strong voice.
Then off Neela flew, to the eye of the storm,
When something around her felt bright and felt warm.

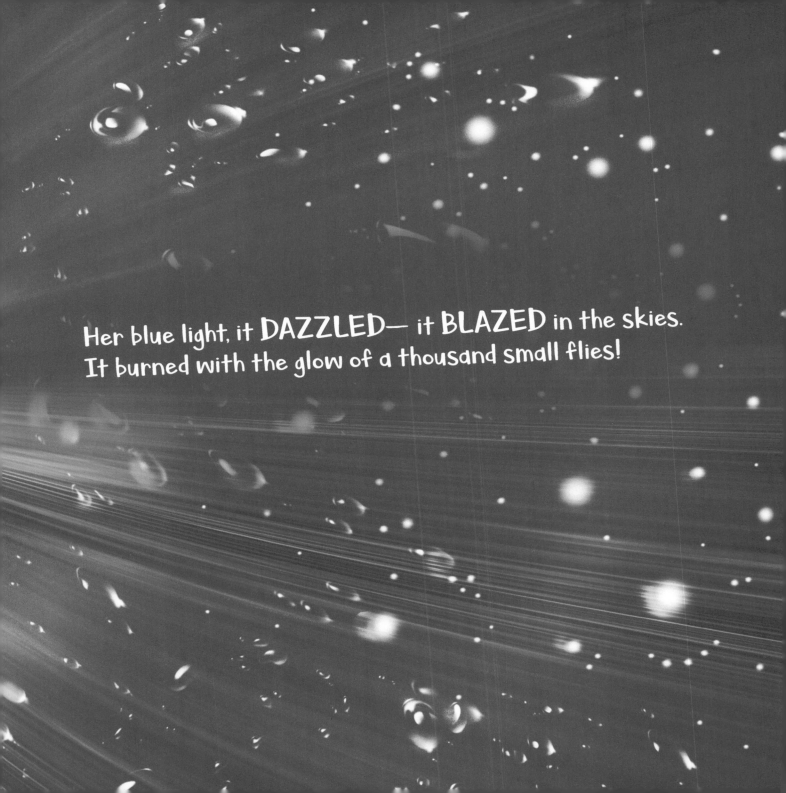

Her blue light, it DAZZLED— it BLAZED in the skies.
It burned with the glow of a thousand small flies!

She zoomed to the rocks and when she was near,
She heard Daniel screaming, "Please, Neela, I'm here!"
She freed frightened Daniel, and with a great flash,
Flew over the lake in one final fast dash.
The moon now shone bright, and the clouds had now cleared.
That once mighty storm was now gone—disappeared!

For once feeling proud, with a head full of hope,
Neela flew over the lake's grassy slope.
But as she looked down, in the water's direction,
She saw something new...

But this time her blue wasn't dull or too pale,
It glowed like a fly who did not fear to fail.
So no longer scared, or too shy to go play,
Neela flew in to now lead the way.

And off they all flew, each one into the night—
Among the bright stars . . . and a brilliant blue light.

CPSIA information can be obtained
at www.ICGtesting.com
Printed in the USA
BVHW011913160223
658686BV00001B/5